The Stubbornly Secretive Servant

Princess Power

The Stubbornly Secretive Servant

By Suzanne Williams
Illustrated by Chuck Gonzales

HarperTrophy®
An Imprint of HarperCollins*Publishers*

The Stubbornly Secretive Servant
Text copyright © 2007 by Suzanne Williams
Illustrations copyright © 2007 by Chuck Gonzales

www.harpercollinschildrens.com

Library of Congress Cataloging-in-Publication Data
Williams, Suzanne, 1949–
The stubbornly secretive servant / by Suzanne Williams ; illustrated by Chuck
Gonzales. — 1st HarperTrophy ed.
p. cm. — (Princess power ; #5)
Summary: When their friend Prince Jonathon disappears, and his servant
refuses to say a word, it takes the help of Princess Tansy's magic flute to discover
his whereabouts.
ISBN-10: 0-06-078306-0 (pbk.) — ISBN-13: 978-0-06-078306-8 (pbk.)
[1. Princesses—Fiction. 2. Princes—Fiction. 3. Friendship—Fiction.
4. Magic—Fiction. 5. Adventure and adventurers—Fiction.] I. Gonzales,
Chuck, ill. II. Title.
PZ7.W66824St 2007   2006028656
[Fic]—dc22   CIP
                                                                         AC

Typography by Jennifer Heuer
❖
First Harper Trophy edition, 2007

To Uncle Max and Aunt Ann

Contents

The Stubbornly Secretive Servant

Crabby Gabby

Princess Lysandra lurched forward as her carriage clattered to a stop in front of a beautiful marble palace. It had been months since she'd visited her big sister, Gabriella. Although Gabriella had often made Lysandra's life miserable with her nagging before she married and moved away, Lysandra soon discovered that she missed her.

Now Gabriella was pregnant and wanted

her sister's company. Lysandra was happy to visit and was excited about becoming an aunt. The baby was due in less than two weeks!

Lysandra was also looking forward to seeing her friends: the princesses Fatima, Tansy, and Elena. Gabriella liked having lots of visitors and had invited them, too. They would be arriving the next day.

As Lysandra climbed down from the carriage, her brother-in-law hurried to meet her. Prince Jerome was a handsome man with fair hair and a strong jaw. Except for a slight hop in his walk and the occasional dart of his tongue, no one would have ever guessed he'd spent nine long years as a frog.

"I'm so glad you're here," said Jerome. "The doctor has confined Gabby to bed, and she's most unhappy about it. Your visit is sure to cheer her up."

It always amused Lysandra to hear him call

her sister "Gabby." If anyone else had dared to use that name, Gabriella would've thrown a fit. Still, as Jerome escorted Lysandra into the palace, her stomach knotted with worry. "Are she and the baby okay?"

Jerome sighed. "The baby's fine, and Gabby is as well as can be expected, I suppose. She's awfully uncomfortable, though. I'm afraid it makes her a bit short-tempered, especially with the palace staff."

Lysandra nodded, somewhat relieved. Gabriella had *always* been a bit short-tempered. If she was really ill, she wouldn't have the energy to nag. "How many people have quit so far?"

Prince Jerome thought for a moment. "Five. No, wait. Seven. I forgot to count the two maids who left this morning."

Lysandra smiled and followed Jerome up the staircase. At the end of a long corridor,

Jerome stopped outside the master bedroom as another maid stormed past them. "Here we are," he said brightly. "You go on in. I'll see you and Gabby later."

"Aren't you coming in too?" Lysandra asked.

"Well, no, I thought maybe I'd—"

"Jerome? Is that you?" Gabriella called.

"I've been waiting and waiting. Is Lysandra here? Do come in at once!"

Jerome sighed. "Coming, dear," he said as he opened the door.

Gabriella propped herself up in bed as they entered. With her golden locks fanned on the pillow behind her, she looked as beautiful as ever.

"Lysandra!" she cried, holding out her arms.

Lysandra ran straight to her sister and gave her a big hug.

"I've missed you so much," Gabriella said. She looked over at Jerome. "Help me up, will you, sweetie?"

Jerome frowned. "Do you think that's wise, Gabby? You know what the doctor said. Standing makes your ankles swell. And it's not good for the baby, either."

Gabriella rolled her eyes. "That doctor! I'd like to see *him* confined to bed for days on end. I bet he wouldn't even last an hour."

"Now, Gabby—"

"Don't you 'Now, Gabby' *me*!" Gabriella exclaimed. "I'm tired of lying down. Besides," she said, her voice softening, "I'll only stay up for a few minutes."

Reluctantly, Jerome helped her out of bed. Once Gabriella was finally standing, Lysandra couldn't help staring at her. "You look like you're hiding a whole Christmas turkey under your gown!"

Gabriella laughed. "Speaking of turkey, I am rather hungry."

"Shall I ask the Royal Chef to send up some supper?" asked Jerome. "Soup and bread, perhaps?"

"Maybe," said Gabriella. "But do you know what I'd *really* like?"

"No, what?"

"Peacock jelly."

Lysandra hid a smile.

"Peacock jelly?" Jerome's brow furrowed. "I've never heard of such a thing."

"Oh, but it's my favorite thing in all the world!" cried Gabriella. "Won't you please go and find some?"

Jerome shrugged. "All right. I'll see what I can do."

As soon as he left the room, Lysandra and Gabriella burst out laughing.

"Ha-ha. *Peacock jelly*," Lysandra repeated gleefully. It was the name of the imaginary food she'd fed her dolls when she was young. But Jerome wouldn't know that, of course. "How long do you think he'll look for it?"

"Long enough for us to have a good chat," said Gabriella.

In truth, Lysandra didn't think Jerome had wanted to stay anyway. He was probably grateful for the opportunity to get away—especially if Gabriella was as short-tempered with him as she was with the palace staff.

"Okay, enough standing," said Gabriella. She took one step toward a chair and grimaced.

Lysandra's forehead wrinkled with worry. "Are you awfully uncomfortable?" she asked, helping her sister to sit down.

Gabriella frowned. "If I'd known how hard this last month was going to be, and that I'd be spending so much time in bed, I might've wanted Jerome to *stay* a frog."

"But you don't honestly mean that, do you?" asked Lysandra.

"Not really. I love Jerome, and I know he loves me. But I'm ready for this baby to be born." Gabriella paused and stretched her feet out in front of her. "This morning I overheard two of my maids talking. They said I was *crabby*. Can you believe it? I gave them both a good tongue-lashing. And then, instead of apologizing, they just up and quit! You don't think I'm crabby, do you?"

Lysandra crossed her fingers behind her back. "No, of course not."

Gabriella smiled. "I'm so happy you're here. Jerome tries to be helpful, but he's so *fussy*."

"I'm glad you invited me," said Lysandra. And since she didn't want to seem fussy too, she vowed to keep her worries about Gabriella and the baby to herself.

Breakfast

THE NEXT MORNING GABRIELLA INSISTED ON having breakfast with Jerome and Lysandra in the Dining Hall.

"I don't think this is a good idea," fretted Jerome as he and Lysandra helped Gabriella down the stairs. "What's wrong with having your meals in bed? We could have breakfast sent up for the three of us."

"I need a change of scenery," Gabriella

whined. "I'm tired of being cooped up in my room."

Though Lysandra sympathized with her sister, she worried that Jerome might be right. She didn't say so, however.

In the Dining Hall, she and Jerome lowered Gabriella into a chair at the table. Gabriella sighed as she gazed out the huge bay window in front of them. "Just look at that view," she said happily.

It *was* beautiful, thought Lysandra, admiring the carefully manicured gardens and the graceful fountains. And in the distance, nestled between tall trees, you could just catch a glimpse of Summer Lake. Jerome and his younger brother, Jonathon, had swum there during their childhoods.

Gabriella signaled to a palace maid. "Please open the window. I'd like some fresh air."

"But Gabby, dear," Jerome protested. "You might catch a chill. And that wouldn't—"

"—be good for me and the baby," Gabriella finished. "Really, Jerome, if you're going to fuss this much *before* the baby is born, I hate to think what you'll be like afterward. Besides," she said, fanning herself with a napkin, "I'm hot."

"You do look warm," Lysandra said, trying to hide her concern. "Your cheeks are flushed."

"It's the extra weight of the baby," said Gabriella, as the maid hurried to open the window. "I'm *always* hot."

"Of course," said Lysandra, relaxing a little.

The serving maid brought in pastries, fruit, bacon, and puffy cheese omelettes, and everyone started to eat. Lysandra was reaching for an apple turnover when her friends arrived, swooping in through the open window on Fatima's flying carpet. Fatima landed just a foot from Jerome—nearly in his lap! As sometimes happened when he became excited or startled, Jerome croaked and hopped out of the way.

"Bats and bullfrogs!" yelled Fatima. She jumped to her feet. "Sorry about that. I didn't

mean to land so close. I thought maybe you'd left the window open for us, so I just flew on in." She peered up at Jerome. "Are you okay? You hopped up there like you were leaping onto a lily pad."

"I'm quite all right, thank you," Jerome said stiffly, taking his seat again. He was very sensitive about his froggy past.

Lysandra and Gabriella hugged the princesses. Elena seemed taller than the last time Lysandra had seen her several months ago. And, if it was possible, Tansy had even more freckles. But as for Fatima, she looked the same as always, dressed in a lovely pink silk blouse and purple pantaloons.

"It's so good to see you all again," said Gabriella. "Lysandra always entertains me with stories of your adventures together."

Elena smiled. "Thanks for inviting us."

"Please sit down," Gabriella said graciously. "Have some breakfast."

"I'd love to," said Tansy, flopping onto a chair.

Fatima shook out a napkin and smoothed it onto her lap. "So, do you see Jonathon often?" she asked. Jonathon was fourteen, only a year older than Fatima.

"He comes for dinner nearly every other

week," said Jerome. "In fact, he'll be here tomorrow, won't he, Gabby?"

Gabriella nodded and reached for another pastry—her *third*, Lysandra couldn't help noticing. Now that she was "eating for two," Gabriella was hungry all the time.

"Is he still studying magic?" Tansy asked. Jonathon had been taking lessons from a wizard when the princesses first met him at Gabriella and Jerome's wedding last year.

Jerome rolled his eyes. "It's all he ever talks about."

"Jonathon transformed a cooking pot into an apple for me the night we met," Fatima said, blushing. "It tasted a bit like iron, but I bet he's gotten a lot better since."

Lysandra exchanged sly grins with Tansy and Elena. They all knew Fatima and Jonathon liked each other.

"He can transform things easily enough,"

said Gabriella. "But he hasn't *quite* gotten the hang of returning them to their original shape." She picked up an ordinary, gray water pitcher from the table. "Jonathon worked his magic on this pitcher the last time he was here. You should've seen him! He spoke some fancy words and waved his arms around. Then the pitcher sprouted four legs and a trunk—and puffed up into the biggest elephant you've ever seen! Of course, I made him change it back right away. I couldn't have an elephant tramping around the palace." She paused. "The re-transformation was *nearly* successful."

Gabriella passed the pitcher to the girls. They examined it but didn't notice anything unusual at first. When they took a closer look, however, they saw that the spout strongly resembled an elephant's trunk.

The princesses began to giggle. "It's a good

thing he hasn't tried to transform *himself*," Lysandra commented.

"I'm sure he's thought of trying," Gabriella said through a mouthful of pastry. "But I think he knows that his parents would be really angry if he did."

Lysandra nodded. Who could blame them for not wanting an elephant for a son? After all, in many ways, their older son was still part frog! On the other hand, she thought, it might be fun to sit on a lily pad or pick up peanuts with your nose once in awhile.

Out and About

AFTER BREAKFAST, WHILE GABRIELLA WAS napping, Lysandra showed the princesses the bedroom they would share during their visit. The large room held four single beds, a wardrobe, and a dresser. Between two of the beds, a window with a wide sill overlooked an apple tree. The fruit-laden branches reached up to the room.

Fatima opened the window and leaned out.

"What lovely red apples!" she cried. "If I hadn't just finished breakfast, I'd eat one right now."

"They're very good," said Lysandra. "You can pick one anytime you'd like."

Standing before the mirror, Elena ran a hand through her tangled hair. "Do you suppose the frizzy look will ever be in style?"

Tansy grinned. "I think your hair is nice."

"Thanks," said Elena. "Too bad it isn't easier to comb."

The girls all knew Elena must miss the beautiful rainbow-colored comb she'd found—and then had to give up—during their last adventure together. Lysandra smiled. She was happy to spend time with her friends again. They took her mind off her worries about Gabriella and the baby.

The princesses spent the morning exploring the palace and the surrounding gardens. Then they flew on Fatima's carpet to a nearby village. In a little shop, Lysandra bought a snuggly blanket for the new baby. She also bought matching blue hair ribbons for her friends. Lysandra paid for the gifts with coins from a magical purse she wore around her neck. A present from her father, the purse refilled itself so that it never went empty.

Back at the palace, the girls ate lunch. Then they unpacked their clothes while Lysandra

checked in on Gabriella. "Did you have a good nap?" she asked.

"No, not really. The baby was kicking me under the ribs." Gabriella groaned. "Besides, I keep having these horrible pains."

Lysandra frowned. "What kind of pains? Should I ask Jerome to summon the doctor?"

Gabriella waved her hand in the air. "Now don't you start fussing too. I'm sure it's just a

touch of indigestion from all the pastries I ate. I don't want Jerome or that mean old doctor to know. They'd say it was because I came downstairs for breakfast, and they'd never let me out of bed again."

"Well, maybe you *should* stay in bed," said Lysandra. "Just to be safe."

"You sound like Jerome! I thought you'd be on *my* side."

"I am," Lysandra said quickly. "But just for today—couldn't you have dinner in your room?"

Gabriella rolled her eyes. "Oh, all right, though I really hate being confined, you know."

"I know, but we'll all come upstairs and eat dinner with you." Lysandra squeezed Gabriella's hand and then showed her the blanket she'd bought for the baby. It seemed to cheer her up some.

Dinner was a simple meal of beef and barley soup, along with homemade bread. A maid brought a large tray to Gabriella's room, and Jerome joined the princesses there. Jerome blew on a spoonful of soup, then flicked up a piece of meat with his tongue.

"*Manners*, Jerome," scolded Gabriella.

"Sorry," he apologized.

The princesses traded amused smiles. Lysandra wondered if, in spite of Gabriella's wishes, Jerome should know about her sister's pains. But Gabriella hadn't mentioned them all evening, so perhaps they really had been nothing to worry about.

Before the girls went to bed that night, they flew on Fatima's carpet to the top of the palace. Hovering over the roof, they gazed at the stars.

"I could stay here all night," Elena said.

"I know what you mean," said Tansy. "Only I'd rather sleep on a comfy bed."

"If you rolled off a bed, you wouldn't have as far to fall, either," Fatima added.

Lysandra laughed. "That's true."

Tansy drew her magic flute from her pocket and began to play a lovely melody. The princesses' thoughts soared through the air, and soon everyone could hear what everyone else was thinking.

I hope Gabriella's baby is a girl, Lysandra thought. *It would be fun to have a niece!*

The stars are so beautiful tonight, thought Elena. *No wonder poets like to write about them.*

I can't wait to see Jonathon again, Fatima thought. Her friends giggled, and she blushed bright red.

Tansy put down her flute and grinned. "Sorry, Fatima. I'll stop playing. I guess some thoughts are better kept private."

"Thank goodness for that," said Fatima.

"The sooner we go to bed, the sooner Jonathon will be here," Lysandra teased.

"Oh, stop it," said Fatima, but Lysandra saw that she was smiling.

At Summer Lake

AFTER BREAKFAST THE NEXT MORNING, LYSANDRA asked her friends if they'd like to go swimming.

"That would be such fun!" exclaimed Elena.

"But I don't know how to swim," said Fatima.

"Oh, that's right," Lysandra said. "No problem, though. The rest of us can teach you!"

Tansy nodded. "You'll love to swim once you know how."

"I suppose it's time I learned," Fatima said with a sigh.

"Great," said Lysandra. "Let's go!"

They changed into bathing suits and grabbed some towels, then flew to the lake. Fatima was a fast learner. In no time at all, the princesses had taught her how to doggie paddle and float. She drifted on her back while the other girls took turns using her flying carpet as a diving board. They did fancy jumps off the carpet as it hovered steadily in the air.

After one of her jumps, Lysandra saw a huge silver trout leap out of the water. It seemed to look right at her before disappearing into the lake with a splash. Lysandra gazed at the spot where the fish had vanished, watching the ripples spread in a circle. A few seconds later, the fish appeared close to

Fatima—and splashed her when its magnificent tail slapped the water.

By now the other princesses had noticed the fish, too. On its next leap, the trout splashed Tansy. She laughed and dove after it, but it was faster than she was and got away.

Again and again the fish leaped and dove, swishing water over the princesses with each successive jump.

"It's playing with us," cried Elena. "I wish we could talk to it."

Tansy frowned. "If I had my flute, we could listen to its thoughts. But I left it in our room because I didn't want it to get wet."

The princesses played with the fish until at last it swam away. Later the wind came up, and they all began to shiver.

"I th-think it's time to go," Lysandra said through chattering teeth. The girls wrapped themselves up in their towels and flew back to the palace.

"When do you think Jonathon will be here?" Fatima asked as they sailed around the apple tree and through the bedroom window.

"I don't know," said Lysandra. "Sometime soon, I imagine."

The princesses dried themselves off and got dressed. Fatima's stomach growled loudly. "Excuse me," she said. "I think swimming makes me hungry."

"Me too," agreed Tansy. "I'm *starving*."

"I'm not sure when dinner will be served," said Lysandra. "We probably won't eat till Jonathon arrives."

Fatima pushed herself up on the wide windowsill. "I'm going to have an apple, if that's okay," she said. "Does anyone else want one?"

"Yes, please," chorused the others.

Moving as nimbly as a monkey, Fatima grabbed onto a branch and swung into the tree. She plucked the apples and tossed them back through the window to Lysandra, who caught them in the folds of her gown.

". . . six, seven, eight!" counted Lysandra. "Enough?"

"Sounds good to me," said Elena. "That's one apiece for now, and four more to eat later."

After Fatima climbed back into the room, Lysandra handed each of her friends an apple. Keeping one for herself, she placed the remaining four on the windowsill.

The apples were sweet and juicy. "Mmm," said Tansy. "Delicious."

"Let's go see Gabriella," Lysandra said after they'd finished their apples. She felt guilty that she hadn't checked in on her as soon as they'd returned from the lake. "Maybe she knows when Jonathon will arrive."

"Wait a second," said Fatima, standing still. "I think I hear something."

The princesses froze.

Tansy cocked her head. "I hear something too. A squeaking sound . . . is that it?"

Fatima nodded.

"Sounds like a rusty hinge," said Elena. "Could it be the door?"

"Let's see," Lysandra said. She pushed the door back and forth, but it didn't make a sound. She shrugged. "Must be something else. We can figure it out later. Let's check on my sister first."

The princesses walked down the hall. As they entered the master bedroom, Gabriella pushed herself up, grunting, and leaned back against her pillows. Her belly stuck out in front of her—round as a crystal ball, only much larger. "Where have you been all this time?" she asked, pouting. "I've been awake for hours and nobody's been to see me."

"I'm so sorry," Lysandra apologized. "We went down to the lake."

"We taught Fatima how to swim," said Tansy.

"And this huge silver trout kept jumping out of the water and splashing us," Fatima added.

Gabriella sighed. "I wish *I* could go swimming."

"You will," Elena said. "As soon as your baby is born."

"Where's Jerome?" Lysandra asked. He could spend more time with Gabriella too, couldn't he?

Gabriella brightened a little. "We've planned a banquet for tonight, with music and dancing afterward in the Grand Hall. Jerome's been making the preparations. And I don't care what the doctor says about staying in bed. I'm coming downstairs to watch." She paused, frowning. "Have you seen Jonathon? I thought I heard horses arrive some time ago. But if it was him, why hasn't he come up to see me?"

"Should he be here already?" Lysandra asked. She hadn't heard any horses, but maybe that was because she'd been too busy talking with her friends. "Do you want us to go look for him?"

Gabriella picked at her bedcovers. "He's usually here by now, and it will be time for the banquet soon. Maybe you'd better go look for him downstairs."

The princesses found Jerome in the kitchen chatting with the Royal Chef.

"No, I haven't seen Jonathon yet," Jerome told them. "Maybe he got a late start. Why don't you use the crystal ball to see what time he left home?"

"Good idea," said Lysandra. She led the others to the room that housed the palace's crystal ball. You could use it to talk to anyone in another castle or palace.

Jerome and Jonathon's mother, Queen Sybil, was sitting at her crystal ball when the princesses looked in on her.

"You mean he's not there yet?" Queen

Sybil asked worriedly. "He left with Thomas, one of our servants, early this afternoon. They should have arrived by now."

"Maybe they stopped somewhere along the way," Lysandra said, not wanting to alarm Queen Sybil. "I bet they'll be here soon."

The queen seemed to relax. "I expect you're right, dear. It's the kind of thing he *would* do. He so likes to explore new places and things."

"Isn't that the truth," said Lysandra. She smiled at Queen Sybil through the crystal ball, but in truth she still felt anxious. What if Jonathon were in some kind of trouble?

Thomas

AFTER THEY LEFT THE CRYSTAL BALL ROOM, the princesses headed upstairs to see Gabriella. When Lysandra told her what they'd learned, she frowned. "I don't understand. Jonathon's never been this late before."

"Why don't we check the stables?" Elena suggested. "If Jonathon *has* arrived, his horse will be there."

"Of course!" cried Lysandra. "I should've

thought of that earlier."

"What does Jonathon's horse look like?" asked Tansy.

Gabriella thought for a moment. "She's dark brown, with a star on her forehead."

The stables were behind the palace. Once outside, the princesses raced down a short cobblestone path to reach them. They checked the horses in every stall. Finally, in the very last stall, they came upon a horse that fit the description. Next to her stood a dusty tan stallion. Both horses were eating companionably from a bag of oats.

A stable boy appeared from around the corner carrying two buckets of water. "Excuse me," Lysandra said, pointing to the dark brown mare. "Can you tell us whose horse this is?"

The stable boy set down his buckets. "The servant who led that mare in—and the dusty tan stallion beside it—said the horses belonged to the prince's own brother."

"The servant must have been Thomas," Fatima said.

Lysandra nodded. "Is he still around?" she asked.

The stable boy shook his head. "He's probably up at the palace."

"Let's go look for him," Lysandra said to her friends.

"Just a second," said Elena. She turned back to the stable boy. "How long ago were these horses brought in?"

The boy rubbed his forehead. "Two, maybe three hours ago."

That would have been while we were still at the lake, thought Lysandra. No wonder they hadn't heard the horses arrive. "Thanks for your help," she said to the stable boy. He nodded and disappeared into one of the stalls.

The princesses looked at one another. "So Jonathon *has* arrived," said Tansy. "Then he's got to be here somewhere."

Elena nodded. "Let's check the palace."

As they walked back along the cobble-stone path, they saw a boy standing near the apple tree. He had his back to them and was peering up into the branches.

"Hey!" Lysandra called. "What are you doing?"

Startled, the boy spun around. He had a thin face, with blue eyes and a narrow nose. Dark, curly hair peeked out from under his gray cap. The boy stared at the princesses, but said nothing.

"What's your name?" asked Tansy.

Instead of answering, the boy took off.

"Wait!" yelled Lysandra. "We just want to talk to you!" The girls ran after him, catching up with him near the front of the palace.

"You wouldn't be Thomas, would you?" asked Lysandra.

The boy nodded, his eyes wide. At last he managed to find his tongue. "I'm a servant in the household of Prince Jonathon, brother of Prince Jerome," he said.

"We know," Elena said gently. "You accompanied Prince Jonathon here, right?"

Thomas nodded again.

"Can you tell us where he is?" asked Lysandra. "We've been searching for him."

"I don't know," Thomas said with a shrug.

"Why did you run away from us just now?" Fatima asked curiously. "What were you doing by that apple tree?"

Thomas shook his head and stared down at the ground. "Can't say."

"Why not?" asked Lysandra. He was the most infuriating boy she'd ever met!

But the servant pressed his lips together

and wouldn't say another word.

Lysandra wasn't sure what to do next. Finally she asked, "Do you promise not to run off while I speak with my friends?"

"Okay," he replied.

The princesses stepped a short distance away. "He must know where Jonathon is," Lysandra whispered. "Why won't he tell us?"

Fatima shivered. "You don't think he's done Jonathon any harm, do you?"

"Oh, I don't think so," said Elena. "Why would he?"

"Maybe it's a practical joke," Tansy suggested. "My brothers are always playing them on me. Jonathon could be in our room this very minute, short-sheeting our beds or something.

He could've left Thomas as a lookout."

"Maybe," Lysandra said doubtfully. Jonathon had never struck her as a prankster. Still, it wouldn't hurt to check.

Taking Thomas with them, the princesses entered the palace and climbed the stairs to their room. As they passed Gabriella's door, Lysandra listened carefully, hoping to hear Jonathon inside. But the room was silent. Gabriella was probably napping again.

The girls continued on down the hall to their room. They hadn't been very tidy. Their wet bathing suits and nightgowns were strewn all around. Thomas looked away, clearly embarrassed.

There was no sign of Jonathon, and nothing in the room seemed to have been touched. Just the same, Tansy turned back the sheets on their beds. They hadn't been touched either. "Guess I was wrong," she said.

"Shh," said Elena. "I hear something."

Everyone fell silent. Lysandra held her breath. There it was again . . . the squeaky sound they'd heard earlier! Then, as if pushed, one of the apples Lysandra had placed on the windowsill mysteriously rolled off. It landed on the floor with a thump.

Searching for Jonathon

THE PRINCESSES RUSHED TO THE OPEN WINDOW. Maybe the boys were playing tricks after all! Lysandra looked down, expecting to see Jonathon grinning up at them. But no one was there.

"The breeze must've knocked it over," Fatima said. She picked up the fallen apple and placed it back on the sill. The squeaky noise had stopped.

"What now?" asked Tansy.

"Let's find Jerome," Lysandra said. Then she caught Thomas's eye. "And I would like you to come with us."

Jerome was in the Grand Hall talking to one of the musicians he'd hired for that evening. Gabriella was there too, sitting in a chair by the fire with her legs stretched out in front of her. The middle of her gown stuck up like a small hill.

"I thought you were in your room napping," said Lysandra.

Gabriella shook her head. "I was tired of napping. Besides, I was hoping to find you." Noticing Thomas, she said, "You're the servant who often comes here with Jonathon, right? Do you know where he is?"

Thomas shuffled his feet. "I'm not sure,

Your Highness."

"What do you mean?" Gabriella asked, raising an eyebrow. "Isn't he with you?"

"I took the horses to the stable," Thomas said, avoiding her stare. "He told me he would meet me by the apple tree."

"How long ago did you arrive?" she asked.

"About two hours ago."

Gabriella frowned. "And you haven't seen Jonathon since?"

Thomas shook his head.

"We left our window open," said Tansy, "and we thought Jonathon might've climbed into our room to play a trick on us. But we checked and he wasn't there."

Gabriella called Jerome over. He questioned Thomas too, but the servant told him nothing more than he'd already told the princesses. Finally Thomas simply clammed up and refused to speak at all.

"I'll organize a search party," Jerome said, his voice sounding grim.

Thomas's eyes lit up. "Please, Prince Jerome. I'd like to be part of it."

"You can't let him go, Jerome," Lysandra said anxiously. "He *says* Jonathon arrived with him, but what if he's lying? I think he knows what happened. Maybe he harmed Jonathon! If you let him go, he might try to escape."

Thomas's face turned red. "I would never harm Prince Jonathon!"

"I'm sorry," Jerome said, "but I think it's best you stay here . . . for now, anyway."

Anger flashed in Thomas's eyes, but he said nothing.

Before Jerome left with the search party, he ordered that Thomas be taken to the tower room. A guard arrived quickly and was

instructed to stand outside the room until
Jonathon was found. As Thomas was led away,
he glowered at Lysandra but remained stubbornly silent.

"You don't *really* think he did anything to
Jonathon, do you?" asked Elena.

"I'm not sure," Lysandra admitted. "But I
do think he knows more than he's letting on."

Fatima and Tansy nodded in agreement.

Jerome bent and kissed Gabriella on the
cheek. "Tell the Royal Chef not to wait dinner. You must go ahead and eat."

"I'm too worried to be hungry," Gabriella
replied.

"Nonsense," said Jerome. "You must try
to eat something. If you don't, it won't be
good—"

"—for me and the baby," finished

Gabriella with a sigh. "I'll try."

Lysandra turned to her friends. "Let's join the search party!"

"Absolutely not," said Jerome. "Suppose we run into danger?"

"We've faced danger before," said Fatima.

Tansy nodded. "Evil cousins, ogres, thieves—"

"That may be true," Jerome interrupted, "but I want you all to stay here and look after Gabriella."

"You act as if I can't take care of myself!" Gabriella exclaimed. She scowled at him. "Besides, there are other people around should I need looking after."

It pleased Lysandra that Gabriella was taking the princesses' side.

But Jerome pursed his lips. "The answer is still no." He turned toward Lysandra. "Let me

be very clear about this: Under *no* circum-
stances are you and your friends to go searching for Jonathon!"

Lysandra fumed silently. Sometimes she
thought she liked Jerome better when he was
still a frog!

The Tower Room

SOON AFTER JEROME LEFT, DINNER WAS SERVED. The maid brought out a magnificent pork roast and a platter of fried trout, too. Bowls of boiled potatoes, green beans with almonds, poached quail eggs, and oranges were also laid on the table. Although she was concerned for Jonathon, Lysandra felt ravenous and piled her plate high. She couldn't help noticing that Gabriella did too, despite her protests to Jerome.

Of all the princesses, only Fatima seemed to have no appetite. "It's going to be dark soon," she said as she picked at her beans. "We should take my flying carpet and search for Jonathon while it's still light. Maybe we'll be able to see him from the air."

"Jerome would have a fit if we went against his orders," said Lysandra. "But perhaps we could try to question Thomas one more time. He *must* have an idea where Jonathon is."

"But wouldn't he tell us if he did?" Elena asked. "He seems just as upset as the rest of us that Jonathon's gone missing."

"That's true," Tansy said, "but it wouldn't hurt to try. Wait, I have an idea! Let's take him a plate of food. Boys are always more willing to talk when their bellies are full."

"Good idea," said Lysandra. Tansy would know about boys and their bellies. She had six brothers, after all. "Would that be okay?" Lysandra asked her sister.

"Of course," said Gabriella. "I was going to send up some food, anyway. Why don't you take a plate for the guard, too?"

The princesses loaded two plates and carried them on trays to the tower room. The guard stood outside the door.

"Thank you kindly, Princess," he said as Lysandra handed him a tray. He jerked his thumb toward the door. "It's been as quiet as a tomb in there. The boy's fast asleep. When I checked a few minutes ago, he was curled up in bed like a baby."

"I bet he'll wake up for food," said Tansy, holding on to the second tray.

The guard unlocked the door, and the princesses stepped inside. It was dark in the room. The only light came from one small window. Squinting, Lysandra could just make out a lump on the narrow bed against the far wall. Thomas had covered himself so completely that even his head was under the blankets.

"Wake up!" Lysandra called to him. "We've brought you some dinner."

But Thomas didn't stir. Lysandra stepped closer to the bed. When she reached down to shake him, she felt something cushiony. Lysandra threw back the top blanket and gasped. Where Thomas should have been, there was a pillow and another blanket, folded to look like a body. The mattress itself was bare, stripped of its sheets.

Lysandra ran to the window. "Look!" she shouted to her friends. Tied to an iron bar under the window was a rope of torn sheets that had been knotted together. The rope

dangled nearly all the way to the ground.

"Bats and bullfrogs!" Fatima exclaimed. "He escaped!"

After telling the surprised guard what had happened, the princesses raced down the steps of the tower. "Thomas is gone!" Lysandra yelled as they burst into the Grand Hall.

Gabriella looked up from her chair by the fire. "What?"

As Lysandra explained, Gabriella's face grew pale. "Then Thomas *must* have done something to Jonathon. Why else would he run away?"

"Maybe he just wants to *find* Jonathon," Elena suggested.

"Then we should catch up with Thomas and follow him," said Lysandra.

"We can take my flying carpet," Fatima said.

The princesses all looked at Gabriella. "As I recall, Jerome only forbid you to search for *Jonathon*, not Thomas," she said with a smile. "So go!"

The girls ran upstairs to get Fatima's carpet. Just before they sailed through the window, Lysandra thought she heard that squeaking sound again. Maybe a mouse was hiding in their room. Well, they would have to look later. Right now they needed to find Thomas—and the faster, the better!

Elena suggested they check the stables before leaving the palace grounds. "Then we'll know if Thomas has taken his horse," she said.

"Great idea," said Tansy.

Jonathon's dark mare was still in her stall, but the dusty tan stallion was missing. "Bats and bullfrogs," muttered Fatima. "He *is* on horseback."

She flew the carpet into the sky and hovered over the palace. From here the princesses could look in all directions: west to the lake, north to the mountains, east to a forest, and south to a broad meadow and the village.

It was nearly dark now and difficult to see, but Lysandra could just make out a dozen lights winding through the forest. "Lanterns," she said, pointing to the flickering glow. "That must be the search party."

"If Thomas is running away, he'll avoid the search party," said Fatima.

"Unless he ran away to *help* with the search," Elena pointed out.

Lysandra shook her head. "I think he knows exactly where to look for Jonathon. He'll search on his own."

"Why don't we head south toward the village," Tansy suggested. "He'll be easy to spot in the meadow if he went that way."

"Sounds good to me," said Fatima. "After all, we've got to start somewhere."

Lysandra nodded in agreement.

Fatima made a sweeping turn with the carpet and the girls sped south over the meadow. The rising moon lit their way.

They'd flown for a few miles without seeing anything when, all at once, they spotted something racing below them. They zoomed closer. "It's just a dog," said Lysandra, disappointed. Then, toward the lake, they heard a horse neigh.

Veering away from the meadow, Fatima steered the carpet west. As the princesses drew near the lake, they spotted Thomas's dusty tan stallion standing at the edge of the water. But Thomas wasn't on him.

Fatima lowered the carpet behind some trees so they'd be well hidden. The girls peered through the darkness, searching for Thomas.

"There he is!" Tansy pointed to a boulder along the shore. Thomas was crouched on the boulder, leaning over the lake. With a sudden splash he jumped into the water and began swimming in circles.

"Jonathon!" he shouted. "Where are you?"

A Nighttime Swim

As Thomas continued to swim in circles, shouting for Jonathon, the princesses stared at one another in shock.

Fatima's face had turned pale. "You don't think Jonathon could have . . . *drowned*?"

Lysandra shook her head. "No, I don't think so. Jonathon is an excellent swimmer! He spent every summer at the lake when he was younger."

"I wonder," Elena said slowly. "Remember that trout? The one that seemed to be playing with us while we were swimming this afternoon? Well, I was thinking about the water pitcher Gabriella showed us. You don't suppose . . ."

"That's it!" Tansy exclaimed. "Jonathon must have turned himself into a fish!"

"He wouldn't," Lysandra protested. "It would be too dangerous." Remembering the fried trout at dinner, she gulped. But those trout were probably caught early in the morning—or even the night before, she reminded herself. *Jonathon as a trout?* It was a ridiculous idea . . . wasn't it?

"We've got to speak to Thomas and make him explain," said Fatima.

Lysandra nodded.

Leaving the cover of the trees, Fatima landed the carpet on shore, and the girls scrambled off.

"Thomas!" Lysandra called to him. "Please get out of the lake!"

Thomas's eyes grew wide when he saw the princesses. He obediently swam for shore. He was soaked from head to foot, and his curly hair hung in wet ringlets.

Lysandra approached Thomas. "Please tell us what's going on," she said. "We're really worried about Jonathon. Why did you think

he would be swimming out here?"

Hugging himself, Thomas shivered in the cool night air. His teeth chattered when he spoke. "I d-don't know. I hoped he would be here, b-but he isn't." His body shook as he looked at them with despair.

"He's cold," said Elena. "We should get

him back to the palace and let him change into warm clothes. *Then* we can talk to him some more."

Thomas gave her a grateful glance.

"All right," Lysandra agreed.

The servant put on his cap, stockings, and boots. Then he mounted his horse.

"We'll follow above you on the carpet," Fatima told him.

When they arrived at the stable, the girls turned their backs while Thomas changed into clean, dry clothes from one of his saddle-bags. With dragging footsteps, he then accompanied the princesses into the palace.

They entered the Grand Hall and looked for Gabriella, but she wasn't there anymore. A servant told them she'd complained of pains and gone up to her room. Jerome was still out with the search party.

Lysandra tensed at the mention of Gabriella's pains, but then dismissed her fear. It was probably just more indigestion. After all, she *had* eaten a lot for dinner. "Let's go find my sister," Lysandra said. "She'll want to hear what Thomas has to say too."

"Come in," Gabriella called when they knocked on her door. The princesses ushered Thomas into her room. "You found him!" she exclaimed.

Hanging his head, Thomas stared at the floor. Lysandra explained where they'd found him and what he'd been doing.

Gabriella turned pale. "You don't think Jonathon *drowned*, do you, Thomas? Is that why you were looking for him in the lake?"

"No, he couldn't have drowned," Thomas said quickly. "Jonathon is a good, strong swimmer."

Gabriella's face regained some color, yet she still looked worried. "You must tell us what you know."

But Thomas clamped his lips together and refused to say another word, no matter what anyone asked. Finally the princesses gave up. Gabriella called for a guard to take Thomas back to the tower room—with instructions that the guard stay *inside* the room this time.

The Squeaky Noise

THE PRINCESSES LEFT GABRIELLA AND WENT
back to their room. As soon as they opened
the door, the squeaky noise started again.

"It must be a mouse," Lysandra said. "I'm
going to find it." At least that was something
she *could* do. Maybe it would take her mind
off Jonathon for a while.

"I'll help," said Elena.

"Me too," added Tansy and Fatima.

Lysandra checked for mouse holes close to the floor, while Elena looked under the beds and shook out the blankets and pillows. Fatima searched the wardrobe, and Tansy rummaged through all the dresser drawers. They found nothing.

"I think the squeaking is loudest over here," Lysandra said, moving toward the window. She looked behind the four apples on the windowsill but still couldn't figure out where the sound was coming from. "I give up," she said at last.

Fatima put her arm around Lysandra, and they stared out the window together. In the distance, the search party's torches still flickered.

"I wonder when they'll give up *their* search?" Lysandra said.

"We mustn't lose hope," Elena said softly.

"I think we need some cheering up," said Tansy. She pulled her magical flute from her pocket and began to play a merry tune. The princesses' thoughts floated through the air. At first they had gloomy thoughts about Jonathon, but after listening to the cheerful music for a while, they began to think of happier things.

Fatima's stomach growled loudly. *I sure am hungry,* she thought. *I should've eaten more dinner.* Blushing, she picked up an apple from the windowsill. "This must be the one that rolled off," Fatima said out loud. "It has a big bruise on it." She shrugged and shined the apple on her blouse. "Oh well. It still looks tasty. I guess I'll eat it anyway."

Just as Fatima was about to take a bite, a tiny voice piped up: *Don't eat me!*

Fatima jumped. "Bats and bullfrogs! Did you all hear that?"

"No, what?" Lysandra asked.

Tansy set down her flute. "Is something the matter?"

Fatima nodded, pointing to the apple. "I could've sworn this apple just talked to me. It

told me not to eat it!"

"You're kidding, right?" Lysandra squinted at the apple. Then she ran her thumb over a round, dark spot on its skin, above the bruise. "Fuzzy," she said, surprised. "Like hair!"

Elena stepped closer and tilted her head. "There's that squeaking noise again. I think it

Don't eat me!

is coming from the apple!"

"You don't suppose . . . ," said Tansy.

"There's only one way to find out," said Lysandra. "Play your flute!"

Tansy lifted her flute to her lips and began to play again.

Lysandra leaned her head closer to the apple. "Is that you, Jonathon?" she asked.

Loud enough for everyone to hear this time, the apple squeaked: *Yes!*

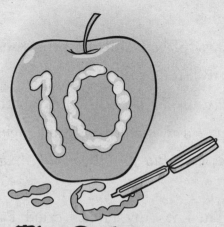

The Return

CAREFULLY HOLDING THE APPLE THAT WAS Jonathon, Fatima placed him on a cushion in the middle of the floor. The four princesses gathered around him.

Tansy studied the apple. "If Jonathon was able to transform himself into an apple, why can't he just change back?"

The apple started to squeak. Lysandra looked at Tansy. "Maybe you should play your flute again so we can understand his thoughts."

Tansy played, and the princesses leaned in close to listen:

I was in the tree, thought Jonathon, *and as long as I was attached to it and growing, I could change back. But then I got picked, and now I'm stuck.*

"Then it's my fault!" cried Fatima. "I'm the one who picked you! I'm so sorry, Jonathon."

No, it's my fault, he thought. *How were you to know?*

Lysandra sighed. "The question is, how can we undo the magic?"

Tansy set down her flute for a moment. "We could try *tying* him onto a branch of the tree. Maybe then he could change back."

"I'm not sure that would work," said Elena. "He still wouldn't be *growing* on the tree."

"How about your magic lotion?" Tansy asked her.

Elena shook her head sadly. "It only works on humans."

"And ogres," Tansy reminded her.

"Mermaids, too," said Fatima.

"Yes," Elena agreed. "But apples aren't much like ogres or mermaids. And my lotion won't *transform* anything. It only heals wounds, like bruises and cuts."

The princesses sat silently, thinking. The apple that was Jonathon sat quietly, too. Lysandra wondered why on earth he had decided to turn himself into an apple. He'd almost been eaten! Well, now he and Jerome had something more in common than just being brothers. Of course, Jerome had been a *frog,* not an apple. If it weren't for Gabriella, he might still be one now. It was her kiss that had broken the spell, after all.

Suddenly Lysandra smiled. Could that magic work on an apple, too?

"Let's try a kiss," Lysandra exclaimed. "It couldn't hurt, right?"

"Who's going to do it?" asked Tansy. "Doesn't the princess have to be fifteen or older for the magic to work?"

"That's what it says in *Courtly Manners and Duties*," Elena said. "But maybe that's only true when kissing frogs."

Lysandra looked at Fatima. "You're the

oldest," she said. "I think you should try. Besides, we all know Jonathon likes you."

The other princesses giggled. Fatima blushed. "Well, okay. . . ." She lifted the apple from the cushion. "I hope this works," she said before planting a kiss on the apple's rosy flesh.

Instantly the apple vanished in a puff of smoke, and Jonathon appeared in its place. The kiss had landed on his cheek.

Turning as red as the apple, Fatima took a step backward.

Jonathon looked rather apple cheeked himself, but he managed a shy grin. "Thanks," he said, brushing a few apple seeds from his shirt.

Lysandra noticed a big bruise on his forearm. "Does that hurt?"

Jonathon nodded, examining the bruise. "Must've happened when I rolled off the windowsill."

"Let me help," said Elena. Taking out her small blue bottle, she poured a dab of lotion into her palm and rubbed it over Jonathon's arm. In a moment the bruise disappeared.

"Was I an apple for very long?" Jonathon asked. "I kind of lost track of time."

"It's been hours," Tansy said. "You missed dinner completely."

"I guess that would explain why it's dark now," said Jonathon, looking out the window. "Say, what are those lights over there?" He pointed at the lanterns, which were moving toward the lake.

"The search party!" Lysandra cried. "We've got to send word to them! And Gabriella will still be worried about you too."

Quickly the princesses shepherded Jonathon out the door and down the hall to Gabriella's room. Gabriella was overjoyed to see Jonathon and hugged him as best she could, given her size and shape. Before she asked him any questions, however, she sent a house servant to call the search party back.

"What about Thomas?" Elena asked.

Jonathon's forehead wrinkled with concern. "Where is he? Poor Thomas will be quite upset. The last thing he knew, I was a fish in Summer Lake."

"What?" exclaimed Gabriella.

The girls exchanged glances. Elena and Tansy had been right about the fish after all, thought Lysandra.

Jonathon sighed. "It's a long story."

"Well, we want to hear all of it," said Gabriella. "But first let's fetch Thomas so that he can hear about your adventure too. Besides, I suspect we owe him a very large apology."

Jonathon's Story

SOON THOMAS WAS BROUGHT TO GABRIELLA'S room. His eyes lit up when he saw Jonathon. "You're back!" he exclaimed. Glancing at the princesses, he frowned. "I didn't tell them anything, Jonathon. Just like I promised."

Jonathon hugged Thomas. "I know. But I was wrong to make you promise." He looked around the room. "You all know some of what happened. I'll try to explain the rest."

Gabriella pushed herself up in bed, and Lysandra sat beside her. The other princesses and Thomas sat on the floor.

Pacing back and forth, Jonathon said, "I've been practicing self-transformation for months now. I knew my parents wouldn't approve, so I kept it a secret." He glanced at Gabriella. "I'm sorry I didn't tell you and Jerome, but I was afraid you wouldn't approve either."

"You're right," Gabriella said. "But go on."

Jonathon sighed. "Thomas was the only one who knew my secret. He just found out a couple of weeks ago, when he saved my life. I'd turned myself into a bird and was happily flying around when a boy threw a rock at me. The rock grazed my arm—my *wing*, that is—and I plummeted to the ground. While I was lying there, a cat crept toward me. . . ."

He paused for a moment. "I really thought that was the end of me. But then Thomas came to my rescue. He raced toward the cat

and chased it away. He didn't know the bird was me at first. I wasn't going to tell him, either, but he figured it out."

Lysandra leaned forward with anticipation. "How?"

Jonathon grinned at Thomas. "You tell it."

"No," said Thomas. "You're better at story-telling." For the first time since his arrival, Thomas smiled. He was rather handsome when he wasn't scowling, thought Lysandra. And he'd stood by his promise to Jonathon even though it made things harder for himself. She felt terrible that she'd misjudged him.

Jonathon continued his story. "Thomas carried me to his room and laid me in a little box. Then he left. I'd recovered enough to transform back by that point, so I did. But Thomas returned before I could sneak away."

"The first thing I saw was the empty box,"

Thomas chimed in. "But what tipped me off were all the feathers stuck to Jonathon's shirt!"

"I swore him to secrecy," said Jonathon. "But, in turn, he made me promise to transform only when he was around to protect me—in case something went wrong."

Gabriella raised an eyebrow. "And today something *did* go wrong."

Jonathon nodded sheepishly. "We had almost reached Summer Lake on our horses this afternoon when we heard voices." He glanced at Lysandra and her friends. "We hid and watched you girls swimming around. Then I decided to have some fun with you, so I . . . well, you already know that part."

"Fatima told me about the big trout that kept splashing them," said Gabriella.

Jonathon blushed. "Exactly. When I told Thomas my plan, he wanted to stay until I transformed back again, but I was afraid you'd hear our horses if they stayed much longer. So I told him to take them along to the stable. I said I would meet him under the apple tree later."

"And until now, that was the last I saw of him," said Thomas.

"I was waiting under the tree for Thomas when I saw Fatima sitting in the window." Jonathon looked at her. "I was afraid you might fall. I thought about calling out a warning, but I didn't want to startle you."

Fatima tossed her head. "You didn't need to worry about *me*. I've had lots of experience sitting on windowsills, and I don't startle that easily. Besides, if I did fall, I'd simply call on my flying carpet to catch me."

"Of course," Jonathon said apologetically. "But I didn't think of that. So I transformed myself into an apple on a branch near the window. That way I could watch to make sure you were safe."

"Apples don't have arms," said Tansy. "How could you have caught Fatima if she did fall?"

Jonathon shrugged. "Usually I can transform back to my human self in an instant."

"But when I plucked you from the tree, you *couldn't* change back," said Fatima.

"I tried to tell you," said Jonathon, "but I could only squeak."

Lysandra laughed. "We thought there was a mouse in our room."

"When you brought Thomas into the room, I used all my strength to roll myself onto the floor," said Jonathon. "I guess I was hoping that somehow he'd realize the apple was me."

"I'm sorry. I assumed you were still a fish," said Thomas. "I thought the wind blew the apple off the sill."

"Of course you did," said Elena. "That's what we *all* thought."

Thomas smiled at her.

"I would've thought the same," Jonathon said quickly. "And if Tansy hadn't played her flute, no one would ever have realized that the apple was me."

Fatima shuddered. "I can't believe I almost *ate* you!"

Before anyone could say anything more, the clatter of horses' hooves below interrupted their conversation. Everyone hurried to the window and looked outside. The search party had returned.

The Dance

THERE WAS A GREAT RUSH OUT THE DOOR TO meet the search party. Lysandra turned back when she saw Gabriella lagging behind. She took her sister's arm and guided her down the stairs. "Thank you," said Gabriella.

They were almost to the Grand Hall when Gabriella let out a moan and stopped walking.

Lysandra clutched her sister's arm. "What's wrong?"

"It's nothing," Gabriella said, but her face had turned pale. "Just another one of those pains I've been having. I'll be all right once I sit down."

"Are you sure?" Lysandra asked anxiously.

"Of course. Now don't fuss."

As Lysandra helped Gabriella into a chair, the search party burst into the Grand Hall. Jerome was so excited to see Jonathon alive and well that he hopped across the room to embrace him.

While Jonathon repeated his story, Lysandra noticed Thomas standing alone near the banquet table. He was looking longingly at a large bowl of fruit. "You didn't have any dinner, did you?" she asked.

"No, Your Highness. I didn't."

"You must be starving," Lysandra said kindly. "The search party hasn't eaten yet, either. I'm sure the Royal Chef is preparing more food. Won't you please have a piece of fruit while you're waiting?"

Thomas eyed her warily, as if he wasn't quite sure he could trust her. Then he plucked a plum from the bowl.

"No apples for you, eh?" Lysandra asked, grinning.

A slow smile crept over Thomas's face. "None that squeak, anyway."

They both laughed. "I'm sorry I suspected you of harming Jonathon," Lysandra said. "I was just so worried about him, but that's no excuse. Was it awful being up in that tower?"

"Not really," said Thomas. "The guard was nice. We played cards together."

Lysandra shook her head. "I shouldn't have been so quick to judge you."

"No harm done, Princess," he replied, biting into his plum.

She pulled her purse from around her

neck and shook out a handful of gold coins. "I'd like for you to have these," she said.

He drew back a few steps. "No, Princess. I couldn't. I haven't done anything to deserve them."

"Please," said Lysandra. "It would make *me* feel better—especially after the awful way I treated you. And besides, you've protected Jonathon so many times."

"Well, all right," Thomas said, taking the coins. "Thanks, Princess."

Lysandra and Thomas walked over to the fireplace, where Jonathon was standing with the search party. Jonathon was just finishing his story as they approached.

"How *did* you shed your apple skin?" one of the men asked.

"Oh . . . um . . . Princess Fatima broke the spell," Jonathon said.

"What did she do?" asked someone else.

Blushing, Jonathon shuffled his feet. "She . . . um . . . *kissed* me."

The men hooted with laughter. "I'd be an apple if it got *me* a kiss," somebody said.

Lysandra rolled her eyes. Sometimes men could be so immature.

Soon the servants arrived with platters of roast pork and potatoes, and the men ate heartily. Afterward Jerome called in the musicians. "Tonight we will dance to celebrate two

things. Our guests," he said, motioning toward the princesses, "and the belated appearance of my brother, Prince Jonathon."

The band struck up a lively tune. Much to everyone's delight, Jonathon asked Fatima to dance. The men from the search party danced with the serving women. Tansy and Elena cornered Thomas and coaxed him out onto the dance floor too. Jerome was talking to the Royal Chef, so Lysandra stood beside

Gabriella. Together they watched the dancers whirl around the room.

"Do you think Jonathon will stop transforming himself after what happened today?" Lysandra asked.

"I doubt it," said Gabriella. "We could forbid it—as could King Mortimer and Queen Sybil, if they knew. But forbidding something only seems to make it more appealing."

Lysandra smiled, thinking of the joy she got from reading under the covers when she was supposed to be asleep.

Gabriella motioned toward the crowd. "You should dance too."

"Maybe later. I'd rather stay here with you."

"Really?" Gabriella looked pleased.

"Really."

Suddenly Gabriella gasped. "Oh my!" She clutched at her belly.

"The pains?" asked Lysandra.

Gabriella nodded, her face stark white.

"I'll get Jerome," said Lysandra. This time Gabriella didn't protest.

A New Arrival

JEROME SENT A MAIDSERVANT TO FETCH THE Royal Doctor. Then he and Lysandra helped Gabriella back to her room. With every third step, she moaned.

After Gabriella was settled in bed, the doctor arrived and examined her quickly. "Why didn't you call me earlier?" he scolded. "This baby is ready to be born!"

"But it wasn't supposed to come for two

more weeks," Gabriella protested weakly.

The doctor raised an eyebrow. "Babies can't tell time."

Glancing at Jerome's worried face, Lysandra wished she hadn't kept Gabriella's pains a secret after all. If anything went wrong with the birth, she'd never forgive herself.

The doctor started to shoo Lysandra out of the room, but Gabriella stopped him. "Please," she said. "I want my sister to stay."

"All right," he said, looking sharply at Lysandra, "but you'll have to make yourself useful."

Lysandra nodded. She'd do whatever the doctor asked.

Jerome kissed Gabriella on the forehead. "I'll wait outside then, shall I, dear?"

The thought of the birth must have made him feel queasy. Lysandra noticed that his skin had turned as green as when he was a frog.

After Jerome left, Gabriella's moans grew louder. The doctor barked at Lysandra to find more sheets. "And send an order down to the kitchen for boiling water," he added.

Lysandra dashed out of the room to ask the housekeeper for water and was back in a

few minutes with an armload of fresh sheets.
The doctor arranged them on the bed and
over Gabriella's knees.

"I'm hot," Gabriella complained. Lysandra
dipped a washcloth into a basin of cold water
and pressed it to her sister's sweaty forehead.

Gabriella thanked her weakly. Her pains were becoming more intense. Between them, Lysandra rubbed Gabriella's shoulders. At last the doctor said, "Here comes the baby."

Gabriella pushed and pushed until finally it was out. Within seconds the baby began to wail.

"Congratulations," said the doctor. "It's a girl!"

Lysandra trembled with excitement. I'm an aunt, she thought. I have a *niece*.

The doctor cleaned up the baby. Then he wrapped her in one of the sheets and handed her to Gabriella. Holding the baby, Gabriella sank back against the pillows—exhausted, but beaming. "Just look at her tiny fingers," she cooed.

Lysandra leaned in close. She stroked the fine golden hairs on top of the baby's head. "Can I hold her for just a minute?" she asked.

"Of course," said Gabriella.

Lysandra held the baby carefully, admiring her long lashes and delicate, button nose. "She's beautiful. Have you decided what to name her?"

"Well, Jerome and I thought about calling her—" Suddenly Gabriella stopped talking, flustered. "Oh my heavens. Jerome hasn't been told about her yet!"

"I'll go get him," said Lysandra. She handed the baby back to Gabriella.

"Joy," said Gabriella, looking into the baby's eyes. "We're going to call her *Joy*."

"Princess Joy," said Lysandra. "It's perfect." She leaned over and kissed Gabriella's cheek. "You're the best sister in the world," she said. Then she ran off to tell Jerome and her friends the good news.

AND NOW FOR A SNEAK PEEK AT

Princess Power #6:
The Gigantic, Genuine Genie

At the Bazaar

PRINCESS FATIMA WAS PRACTICING LOOP-THE-loops on her flying carpet when she spotted three carriages. They were climbing up the long, tree-lined drive to her parents' palace. Giving a whoop, she dove toward the ground, pulling up at the last second to land neatly beside the front gardens. No sooner had she landed than the carriages clattered to a stop. Fatima's friends—the princesses Lysandra,

Tansy, and Elena—flung open the doors and leaped out.

"Welcome!" said Fatima, hugging them each in turn. "I'm so glad you could come."

Tansy stared at the black marble palace in front of her. "Wow!" she exclaimed. "This place is *huge*."

Fatima smiled. The castle Tansy and her six brothers lived in was small, but it had seemed cozy to Fatima.

In a few minutes, servants arrived to carry the princesses' bags into the palace. "I know you just got here," said Fatima, "but I wonder if you'd like to fly into town and shop at the bazaar. It closes in a couple of hours, though. So if you want to see it, we should go there first thing."

Lysandra brushed back her blond waves. "I'd love to see it. There's something I'd like to look for."

"Sounds good to me," said Tansy.

"Me, too," Elena agreed.

Fatima grinned. "Then let's go!"

The princesses settled onto the flying carpet. Fatima pulled up on the front edge, and the carpet rose into the air.

"Whee!" said Lysandra. "I just *love* flying."

The girls followed the tree-lined drive until they came to a river that flowed past small, flat-roofed houses. In the distance the striped tents of the bazaar billowed up like sheets flapping on a clothesline.

"Wow!" said Tansy. "I can't wait to see what's under those tents."

Fatima landed the carpet just outside the bazaar. The princesses scrambled off, and Fatima rolled up the carpet and strapped it onto her back. "This way," she said, leading them under the tents.

The girls joined the throng of people

winding their way past displays of beautiful copper trays, leather bags, woven tablecloths, and decorated pots. The shouts of merchants hawking their wares blended with bawling camels and chattering monkeys atop their master's shoulders.

The princesses stopped to look at some necklaces. A silver-and-turquoise one caught Fatima's eye. She tried it on. "Pretty," she said, admiring herself in a mirror. "What do you think, Lysandra?"

But Lysandra didn't reply.

Fatima looked around but couldn't see her anywhere. Panicking, she called to Tansy and Elena, who were also trying on necklaces. "Quick! Lysandra must have wandered away. We've got to find her before she gets lost!"

Find out what happens in the next Princess Power adventure!

Check out more
Princess Power adventures!

Princess Power #1: The Perfectly Proper Prince

Princess Lysandra finds sewing, napping, and decorating the palace to be extremely boring. She wants adventure! So when Lysandra meets Fatima, Elena, and Tansy, she couldn't be happier. But their first quest comes even sooner than expected, when they stumble upon a frog that just *might* have royal blood running through his veins.

Princess Power #2: The Charmingly Clever Cousin

Princess Fatima doesn't care much for her brother-in-law, Ahmed. His cousin Yusuf is much more charming, with his elegant mustache and impressive magic tricks. Yet when Ahmed goes to visit his dying father—and never returns—Fatima starts to worry. Something suspicious is going on, and it just might be up to the princesses to come to the rescue!

Princess Power #3: The Awfully Angry Ogre

...ble occurs in her ...hallenges him is ...forbidden to fight ...d her friends save

Princess Power #4: The Mysterious, Mournful Maiden

Princess Elena is excited to find a treasure on the beach—a beautiful comb that tames and softens her frizzy hair. However, she soon starts dreaming of a green-haired maiden who cries that she can't live without her comb. The princesses all want to help. But will they be able to find the maiden . . . before it's too late?

Princess Power #5: The Stubbornly Secretive Servant

The princesses are having a ball visiting Lysandra's sister, Gabriella, and brother-in-law, Jerome. And they can't wait for Jerome's handsome brother, Prince Jonathon, to join them. But when he never arrives, everyone panics. They must find the missing prince—without the help of his stubborn servant, Thomas, who's not saying a word!

🔺 HarperTrophy®
An Imprint of HarperCollinsPublishers   www.harpercollinschildrens.com